Dedicated to the memory of Gyo Fujikawa
and her influence on children's literature.
And to all the makers. —D.D. & M.D.

Katherine Tegen Books is an imprint of HarperCollins Publishers.

To Make

Text copyright © 2022 by Danielle Davis

Illustrations copyright © 2022 by Mags DeRoma

All rights reserved. Manufactured in Italy.

ISBN 978-0-06-308406-3

The artist used all kinds of art supplies from graphite to pastels to gouache, paper, and glue, and a fair amount of waiting (for the paint to dry, of course) to create the illustrations for this book.

Typography by Mags DeRoma and Molly Fehr

22 23 24 25 26   RTLO   10 9 8 7 6 5 4 3 2 1

First Edition

to make

Words by DANIELLE DAVIS   Pictures by MAGS DeROMA

 KATHERINE TEGEN BOOKS
An Imprint of HarperCollins Publishers

To make a cake,

gather,

make,

To make a garden,

gather,

make,

To make
a song,

gather,

wait.

Keep making.

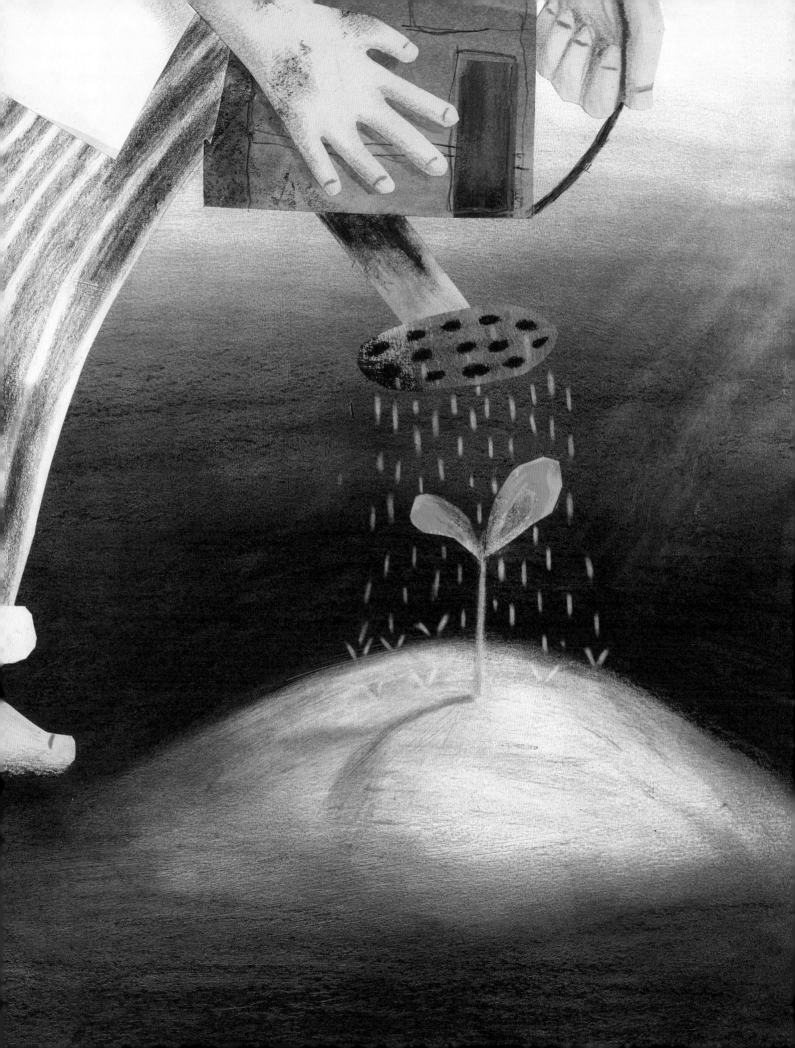

Keep waiting.

To make
a plan,

gather,

To make
a story,

gather,

wait!

To make
a friend,

gather,

make,

wait.

keep making.

Keep waiting.

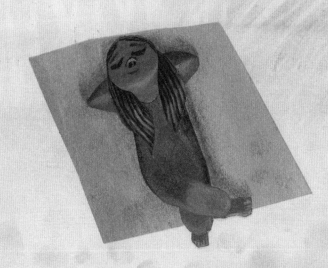

To make
a poem,

a painting,

a sweater,

a city,

a dance,

a fort,

gather,
make,
wait.

Sometimes you will make

and make

and make

and wait

what feels
like forever,

But keep making.

Keep waiting.

Because one day you will
share something wonderful

that only you
know how to make.